AF228628

FACT AND FICTION OF THE CIVIL WAR

BY RYAN GALE

CONTENT CONSULTANT
Larry E. Hudson, PhD
Associate Professor of History
University of Rochester

Core Library

An Imprint of Abdo Publishing
abdobooks.com

Cover image: Ulysses S. Grant was the Union commanding general.

abdobooks.com

Published by Abdo Publishing, a division of ABDO, PO Box 398166, Minneapolis, Minnesota 55439.
Copyright © 2022 by Abdo Consulting Group, Inc. International copyrights reserved in all countries.
No part of this book may be reproduced in any form without written permission from the publisher.
Core Library™ is a trademark and logo of Abdo Publishing.

Printed in the United States of America, North Mankato, Minnesota
052021
092021

Cover Photo: John Parrot/Stocktrek Images/Getty Images
Interior Photos: Everett Collection, 4–5; Everett Collection/Shutterstock Images, 6, 17, 43; Red
Line Editorial, 9, 37; Duke University Libraries/Internet Archive, 11; North Wind Picture Archives,
14–15, 30–31; New York Public Library, 18, 25; Calla Kessler/The Washington Post/Getty Images,
22–23; Library of Congress, 27; MPI/Archive Photos/Getty Images, 33, 45; Currier & Ives/Library of
Congress, 34

Editor: Aubrey Zalewski
Series Designer: Ryan Gale

Library of Congress Control Number: 2020948168

Publisher's Cataloging-in-Publication Data

Names: Gale, Ryan, author.
Title: Fact and fiction of the civil war / by Ryan Gale
Description: Minneapolis, Minnesota : Abdo Publishing, 2022 | Series: Fact and fiction of American
　　　history | Includes online resources and index.
Identifiers: ISBN 9781532195112 (lib. bdg.) | ISBN 9781098215422 (ebook)
Subjects: LCSH: United States--History--Civil War, 1861-1865--Juvenile literature. | United States-
　　　-Politics and government--19th century--Juvenile literature. | Truthfulness and falsehood--
　　　Juvenile literature. | Public opinion--Juvenile literature.
Classification: DDC 973.7--dc23

CONTENTS

SECESSION AND THE CIVIL WAR

O n December 17, 1860, South Carolina's delegates gathered in a church. The church was in the state capital, Columbia. A banner hung from the ceiling. It read, "South Carolina Convention of 1860." Convention president David F. Jamison stood up to speak. He said the people of South Carolina were unhappy with the US Constitution. The Constitution lists the country's laws and people's rights. It also gives states the right to make their own laws.

In November 1860, people of South Carolina met and decided to hold a state convention on secession from the United States.

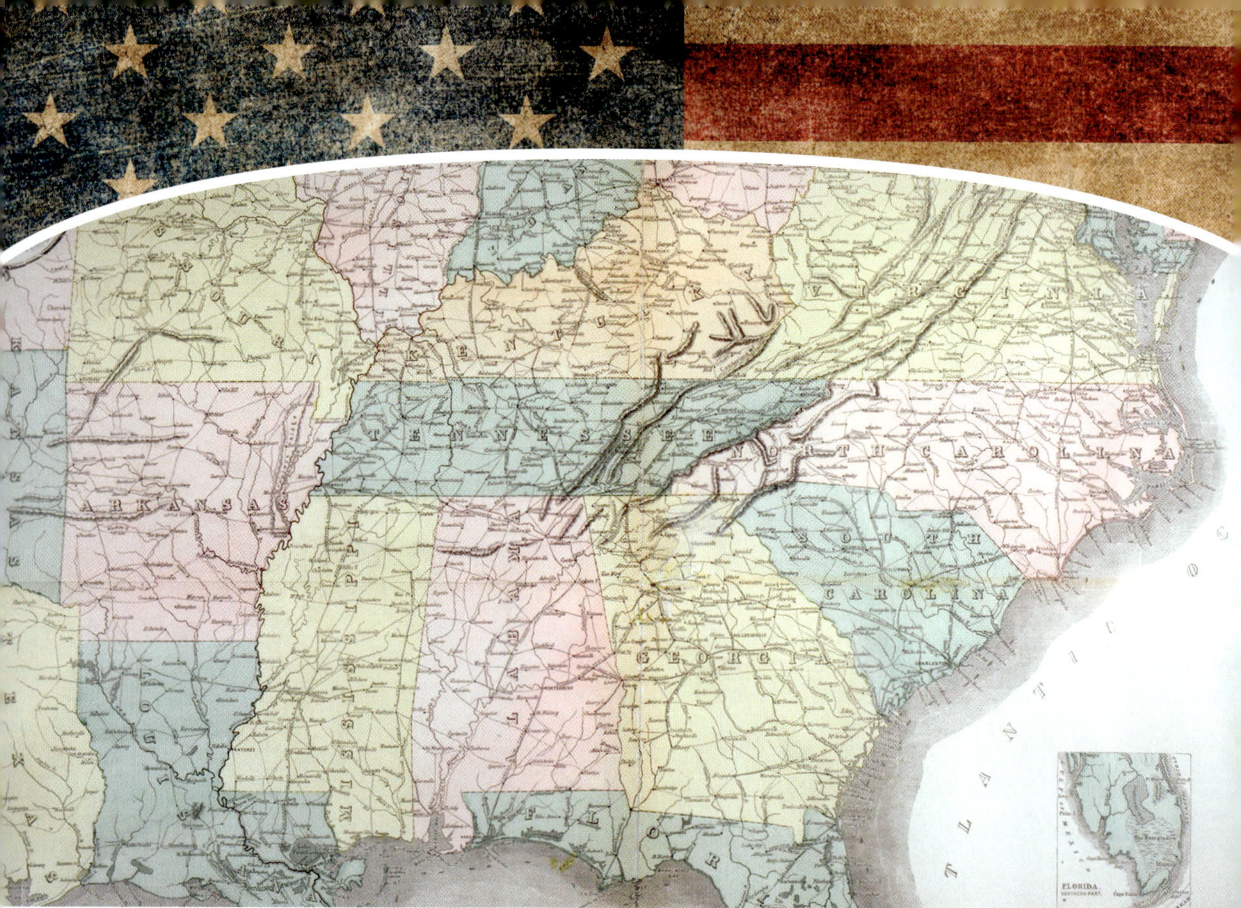

The Southern states formed the Confederate States of
America (CSA).

Jamison said the federal government was not
serving the people of South Carolina. South Carolina's
state laws supported the enslavement of Black people.
But the federal government limited slavery. Jamison
said the people of South Carolina should be free from
the US government. On December 20, the people
voted. One hundred sixty-nine delegates voted to

secede. They wanted to leave the United States. No one voted to stay.

Ten other Southern states left the Union after South Carolina. They were Mississippi, Florida, Alabama, Georgia, Louisiana, Texas, Virginia, Arkansas, North Carolina, and Tennessee. Together they formed the Confederate States of America (CSA). The states that made up the CSA all had one thing in common. Slavery was legal there. It was illegal in most states in the Union. However, some slave states did not leave. These states were on the border between the North and South. They included Maryland,

SLAVERY IN AMERICA

Enslaved people were first brought to the American colonies in the early 1600s. Colonists forced them to work on farms. Many men and women were taken from Africa. Others were born into slavery. By 1830, the Southern states depended on slave labor to grow food and crops, such as cotton and sugar. In 1860, there were nearly 4 million enslaved Black people in the United States.

Delaware, West Virginia, Kentucky, and Missouri. West Virginia became a state in 1863, during the war. Within these states there was support for both sides.

The American Civil War was fought between the United States, or the Union, and the Confederacy. It took place between 1861 and 1865. It claimed the lives of more than 750,000 people. It left much of the South in ruins. In the end, the Confederates were defeated. The Union was saved.

For years, some teachers and historians have taught that the South seceded over states' rights. Others have taught that the South left over the issue of slavery. People wonder which is fact and which is fiction.

SLAVERY AND SECESSION

Some Southern states claimed that they seceded to keep their rights. Four of the 11 issued statements to the federal government listing their reasons for leaving. In the documents, the states claim to have been treated unfairly by the federal government. The statements

CIVIL WAR
SURVEY

The social justice organization Teaching Tolerance surveyed 1,000 high school seniors in the United States in 2016. The survey asked students what caused the Civil War. Their answers are shown in the pie chart below. Most did not give the correct answer of "preserve slavery." What does this chart show about students' understanding of the Civil War?

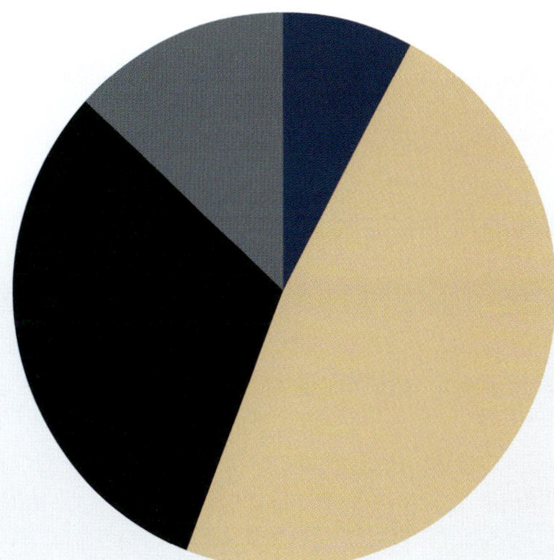

 Preserve slavery: 8%

 Protest taxes on imported goods: 48%

 Other: 31%

 Not sure: 13%

Source: "Teaching Hard History: American Slavery." *Southern Poverty Law Center*, 2018, splcenter.org. Accessed 10 Aug. 2020.

mention the issue of slavery several times. And it's
clear that the states wished to protect the institution of
slavery. Many Southern politicians didn't like that other
states passed laws against slavery. The Confederate
Constitution banned its member states from passing
laws that restricted slavery.

After the Civil War, some former Confederates
tried to change peoples' views of events. They wanted
Americans to believe that thousands of people had
fought and died for a good cause. They did this by
saying Confederates had fought for states' rights and
freedom for white people in the South. This made
them look like heroes instead of rebels. They also
said that Black people were content being enslaved.
Confederates claimed that enslaved people even
fought for the Confederacy. Many people believed
these sentiments. Some even built monuments to honor
Confederate leaders. Over time, this information found

The Confederacy adopted its Constitution on March 11, 1861.

CONFEDERATE CONSTITUTION.

WE, the people of the Confederate States, each state acting in its sovereign and independent character, in order to form a permanent federal government, establish justice, insure domestic tranquility and secure the blessings of liberty to ourselves and our posterity—invoking the favor and guidance of Almighty God—do ordain and establish this constitution for the Confederate States of America:

ARTICLE I.

SECTION 1.

All legislative powers herein delegated shall be vested in a congress of the Confederate States, which shall consist of a senate and house of representatives.

SECTION 2.

1. The house of representatives shall be composed of members chosen every second year by the people of the several states; and the electors in each state shall be citizens of the Confederate States, and have the qualifications requisite for electors of the most numerous branch of the state legislature; but no person of foreign birth, not a citizen of the Confederate States, shall be allowed to vote for any officer, civil or political, state or federal.

2. No person shall be a representative who shall not have attained the age of twenty-five years, and be a citizen of the Confederate States, and who shall not, when elected, be an inhabitant of that state in which he shall be chosen.

3. Representatives and direct taxes shall be apportioned among the several states, which may be included within this Confederacy, according to their respective numbers, which shall be determined by adding to the whole number of free persons, including those bound to service for a term of years, and excluding Indians not taxed, three-fifths of all slaves.

its way into books, movies, and television shows. It even exists in some school textbooks.

FACTS AND FICTION

The reasons for the American Civil War are just one commonly misunderstood part of the war. Facts about the war have been misunderstood and exaggerated over the years. Doing a little more research can give people a better understanding about this influential time in American history. They can find the truth for themselves.

STRAIGHT TO THE
SOURCE

News is not always accurate. Journalists during the Civil War often viewed events from a distance. Or they recorded the events from witness accounts. The *Philadelphia Daily Evening Bulletin* was a Northern newspaper. A journalist for the newspaper wrote in 1861:

> *We are living history in these exciting times, and the historians are the newspaper writers, reporters and correspondents. To be sure, some of them make mistakes at times, and each day's paper is not always an exactly accurate record of each day's events. . . . The very sheet which we print today, may at a future time be closely scanned by some patient student, in his search for the actual facts concerning the mad attempt at revolution got up by some of the Southern States.*

> Source: Paul Farhi. "How the Civil War Gave Birth to Modern Journalism in the Nation's Capital." *Washington Post*, 2 Mar. 2012, washingtonpost.com. Accessed 10 Aug. 2020.

WHAT'S THE BIG IDEA?

Take a close look at this passage. What is the main connection being made between journalism and the Civil War? What point is the author making about recording history? Why do you think the author talked about making mistakes? What does this suggest about historical research?

CHAPTER TWO

THE US ARMY

There are many myths about the Civil War. These myths range from soldiers' experiences to their reasons for fighting. Some say that military surgeons did not use anesthesia. Anesthesia is a medical treatment. It keeps someone from feeling pain. Movies often show Civil War soldiers biting down on sticks or lead bullets to get through surgery. In reality, anesthesia was used in approximately 95 percent of surgeries during the war. Another myth is about who fought in the Civil War. Some say soldiers in the war were all born in the United States. In fact,

More than 2.1 million soldiers fought for the United States in the Civil War.

both armies contained thousands of immigrants from Mexico, Canada, and Europe.

SAVING THE UNION

There is also a myth about why the United States fought. Many people believe that the US government's main goal was to end slavery. Other people believe that the government didn't want to end slavery at all. In 1861, Congress stated that the government's goal for the war was to save the Union, not to end slavery.

In November 1860, Abraham Lincoln was elected president of the United States. In Lincoln's first speech as president, he said that he did not plan to interfere with slavery where it existed. President Lincoln was against slavery. But he thought it was the president's duty to preserve the Union, not to end slavery. Yet Lincoln's views on slavery influenced many of his actions. On the eve of the Civil War, Southern politicians offered Lincoln a chance to prevent a war. But they said he must protect slavery forever. Lincoln rejected their offer.

Abraham Lincoln was the sixteenth president of the
United States.

When the war began, Lincoln tried to keep his
promise not to interfere with slavery. He didn't want
to upset people in the Union's slave states. He was
afraid they would join the Confederacy. In May 1861,

Historical images showed thousands of Black people fleeing to US military camps to escape slavery.

thousands of enslaved refugees began flooding into US military camps. The military had to take care of them. US soldiers began seeing how enslaved people were mistreated. They also began working and fighting alongside Black people. These experiences changed some soldiers' views on slavery. They wanted to end slavery because it was the right thing to do.

EMANCIPATION

Lincoln used this change in opinion to turn his personal feelings on slavery into public policy. He issued

the Emancipation Proclamation. It outlined the US government's new official war policy to end slavery. It went into effect on January 1, 1863. This was partly a military measure. Ending slavery hurt the South's ability to wage war. Foreign countries that were against slavery couldn't assist the South. But it was also a step in Lincoln's plan to end slavery

EMANCIPATION PROCLAMATION

The Emancipation Proclamation only freed enslaved people in the Confederate states. It did not free enslaved people in the loyal border states. Nor did it free people in Confederate territory that was under US control. It also didn't make Confederates release enslaved people. This was because the Confederates no longer recognized US authority. However, the proclamation was backed by the US military. US armies would free enslaved people in the Confederacy where they found them. The US military would also fight to keep them free.

in the United States. It gave US soldiers a cause to fight for. It also gave Black people the chance to join in the fight. It allowed them to serve as soldiers in the US Army. Thousands joined, and the war became a fight for freedom.

At the war's start, the US government's goal was not to end slavery. But its goals changed during the war. The Emancipation Proclamation paved the way for the Thirteenth Amendment to the US Constitution. The Thirteenth Amendment officially ended slavery in the United States in 1865.

STRAIGHT TO THE
SOURCE

In August 1862, President Lincoln wrote a letter to an editor of the *New-York Daily Tribune*. The letter expressed his views on the Civil War and slavery. It read:

> *My paramount object in this struggle is to save the Union, and is not either to save or to destroy slavery. If I could save the Union without freeing any slave I would do it, and if I could save it by freeing all the slaves I would do it. . . .*
>
> *I have here stated my purpose according to my view of official duty; and I intend no modification of my oft-expressed personal wish that all men every where could be free.*

Source: Abraham Lincoln. "Abraham Lincoln to Horace Greeley." *Daily National Intelligencer*, 23 Aug. 1862. *Library of Congress*, loc.gov. Accessed 28 Aug. 2020.

WHAT'S THE BIG IDEA?

Take a close look at this passage. What is the main point that Lincoln is making in his letter? What details does he provide that support that main point?

BLACK PEOPLE IN THE CONFEDERACY

There are many monuments at Arlington National Cemetery in Virginia. Only one is dedicated to Confederate soldiers. Among the figures on the monument is a Black man in a Confederate uniform. People have claimed that thousands of free and enslaved Black people fought as soldiers in the Confederate army. They use photographs of Black people in Confederate uniforms as evidence. They refer to Black people listed on military payrolls. They also

The Confederate Memorial at Arlington National Cemetery was built in 1914 by artist and former Confederate soldier Moses J. Ezekiel.

point to those who received military pensions. But in reality, few Black people fought for the Confederacy.

PERSPECTIVES

SLAVE LABOR

Thousands of white Southerners left their jobs to fight in the war. Enslaved people filled these jobs. Black people were forced to work in factories, mines, hospitals, warehouses, and shipyards. Joseph E. Brown was the governor of Georgia in March 1863. He said, "The white labor of the South is under arms to sustain slavery, as well as our other interests, and the labor of the slaves must be employed to sustain our white men in the field and their families at home."

MILITARY LABOR

The Confederate military didn't allow Black people to fight until 1865. But it did use them for noncombat jobs. The military forced thousands of enslaved people to build forts, dig trenches, and work as cooks and nurses. When armies moved, enslaved workers traveled with them.

Historical images depicted enslaved Black people who were forced to work for the Confederate military. Historical images often depicted stereotypes of Black people.

THE FIRST LOUISIANA NATIVE GUARD

In 1861, some free Black men in New Orleans, Louisiana, purchased weapons and uniforms. They formed a militia known as the First Louisiana Native Guard. Militias were groups of citizens who defended cities or states. The men of the Native Guard wanted to protect their homes and social standing. Many militias joined the Confederate army, but the Native Guard did not. Less than one year later, a law was passed that banned anyone who was not white from serving in a militia. The militia was broken up. Some of its members later fought for the United States.

As many as 10,000 enslaved people traveled with the 70,000-strong Army of Northern Virginia. Observers sometimes mistook these enslaved people for soldiers.

Enslaved workers often had their names entered into military payroll records. This allowed them to receive supplies from the military. But this did not mean they were soldiers. In fact, the payrolls often listed their occupation as laborers.

Confederate soldiers were sometimes photographed with their enslaved servants.

Some Confederate soldiers brought enslaved people with them to war. Enslaved servants did laundry, cooked, and took care of equipment for their enslavers. Some even had military uniforms. Photographs of these Black men in uniform have led some to believe that they served as soldiers. Often, they were photographed sitting or standing next to the white people who had enslaved them. Some held weapons. But these weapons likely did not belong to them. Some historians believe the weapons were only props. The prop weapons did not indicate that the men were soldiers.

Many Confederates were afraid that enslaved people would revolt if given weapons. So the Confederacy made it illegal for Black people to serve as soldiers. But the Confederacy was near defeat in March 1865. It needed more soldiers. Only then did it agree to let Black people fight. Very few joined the Confederate army. Those who did never received weapons. They didn't even see battle before the fighting ended a few weeks later.

Some Black people received military pensions after the war. These pensions are payments made to soldiers after they leave the military. They are rewards for military service. The US government gave pensions to many US soldiers but not to former Confederate soldiers. Southern state governments began offering these pensions in the late 1860s. In 1888, Mississippi began extending these pensions to Black people. Other Southern states did not offer pensions to Black people until the 1920s. More than 2,500 Black people received pensions from former Confederate states. Usually, only soldiers get military pensions. This has led some people to believe that Black pensioners had been Confederate soldiers. But pension applications usually listed a person's job in the military. Jobs listed on most Black peoples' applications show that they were enslaved workers.

FURTHER EVIDENCE

Chapter Three discusses Black people in the Confederate army. What is the main point of this chapter? What key evidence supports this point? The website below offers more information on the topic. Does it support the evidence presented in this chapter? Does it add any new evidence?

MYTHS AND MISUNDERSTANDINGS: BLACK CONFEDERATES

abdocorelibrary.com/fact-fiction-civil-war

BATTLES OF THE CIVIL WAR

Many important events of the Civil War took place in Maryland, Virginia, and Pennsylvania. These states were part of the Eastern Theater. Authors have written thousands of books about the events there. Most movies about the war also focus on these events. This has led many people to believe that the war only took place in the East. But there were three theaters in the war. The Eastern Theater covered the land between the Appalachian Mountains and the Atlantic Ocean. The Western Theater was

Richmond, Virginia, was the capital of the CSA.

the area between the Appalachian Mountains and the Mississippi River. And the Trans-Mississippi Theater was West of the Mississippi River. Events in the Western Theater had major impacts on the war. Some historians believe that they were even more important than events in the East.

The East certainly played a critical part in the Civil War. Virginia was one of the most populated states in the South. Its capital, Richmond, was the capital of the Confederacy. Virginia was also the closest Confederate state to the US capital. And the largest Confederate armies were stationed in that area. For these reasons, Lincoln and many of his military leaders saw Virginia as the most important military target.

The Western Theater was the agricultural center of the Confederacy. It was an important source of corn, rice, and wheat. Sugar and cotton grew there. It also had cattle and horses. The region covered an area roughly the size of France. It included the states

US soldiers overtook New Orleans in 1862. New Orleans was an important Confederate port in the Western Theater.

of Kentucky, Tennessee, Missouri, Georgia, Alabama, Mississippi, eastern Louisiana, western Florida, and the Carolinas. It contained New Orleans, Louisiana, the largest city in the Confederacy. It also had important railroads, ports, and factories.

FIGHT FOR THE MISSISSIPPI

A war between the United States and the Confederacy seemed inevitable in the spring of 1861. So US general Winfield Scott developed a plan to win. His plan was to use the US Navy to block off the Atlantic coast. He also

US gunboats attacked Confederate forts along the Mississippi River during the Civil War.

planned to use gunboats and soldiers to take control

of the Mississippi River. Scott's plan was nicknamed

the Anaconda plan. An anaconda is a type of snake.

The plan would squeeze the Confederacy as a snake

squeezes its prey. The Anaconda plan never happened.

However, President Lincoln eventually combined Scott's plan with his own plan to invade the South.

The main focus in the Western Theater was the Mississippi River. It was an important transportation route for the Confederacy. If US forces took the river, they would cut the Confederacy in two. This would stop the flow of food and crops from moving west to east. It would also keep Confederate soldiers and supplies from reaching armies in the East. The war in the Western Theater was a success for the United States. US forces had control of the entire Mississippi River by the summer of 1863.

BATTLES OF THE WESTERN AND TRANS-MISSISSIPPI THEATERS

Many of the largest and most famous battles did take place in the East. Some of these were Bull Run, Antietam, Gettysburg, and Petersburg. But several important battles also took place in the Western and Trans-Mississippi Theaters. These included the Battle of Pea Ridge in 1862. The Battle of Pea Ridge secured Missouri for the US Army. Another battle was the Siege of Vicksburg in 1863. It secured the lower Mississippi River. And in 1864, the Battle of Atlanta captured the Confederacy's important railroad and supply center.

Victories in the Western and Trans-Mississippi Theaters helped strengthen morale in the US Army. They also helped keep public support for the war. The support offset US defeats in the East. The US Army's capture of Atlanta, Georgia, boosted Lincoln's approval ratings at a key time. It helped him win reelection in 1864. The election was a major blow to Confederates. They had hoped a new president would end the war and keep slavery. Once the war in the West was won, the western US forces joined those in the East.

EASTERN BIAS

Events in the Western and Trans-Mississippi Theaters were important to the outcome of the war. But they are fairly unknown today. The West was not as developed as

CIVIL WAR
THEATERS

The map below shows the three theaters of the Civil War. It also marks some of the major battles. What do you notice about where the battles were located? How does seeing the map help you understand the importance of the Western Theater?

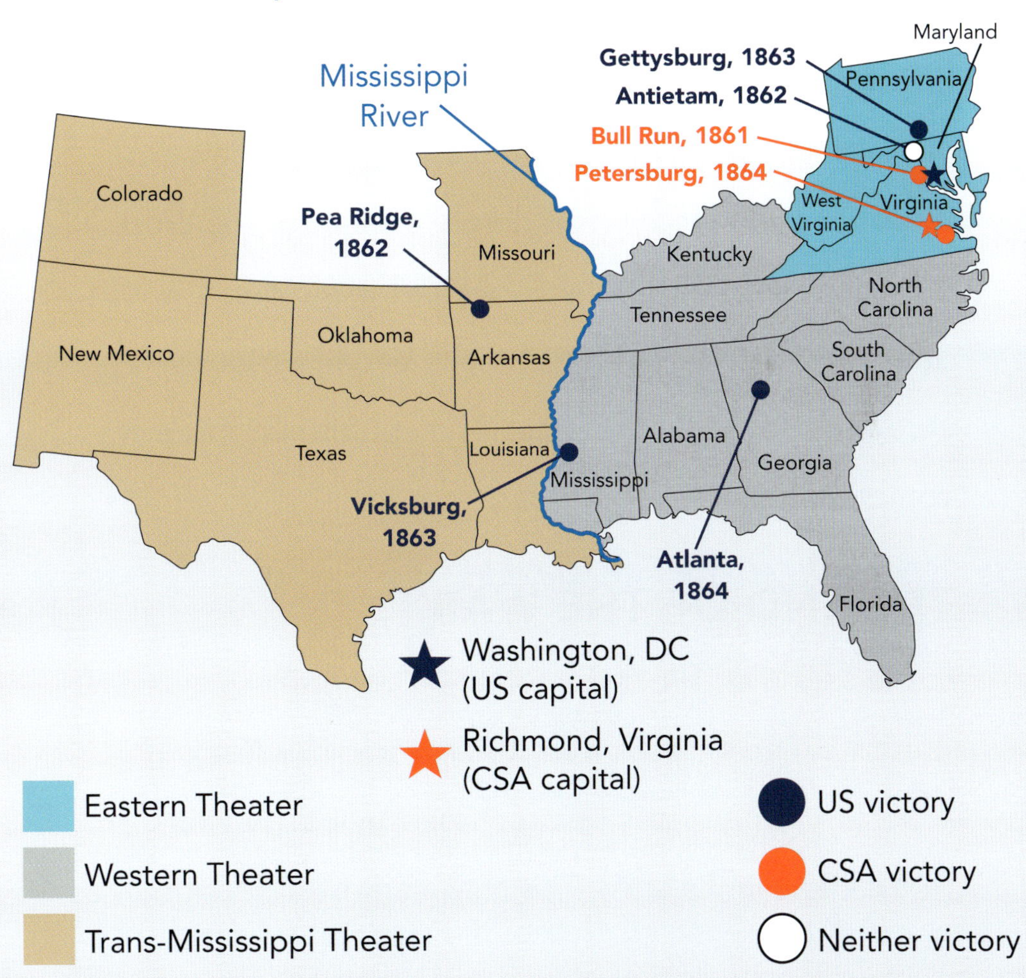

the East in the 1860s. It had a much smaller population. It had far fewer journalists covering the war. Journalists from popular Eastern newspapers did not want to write about events in the West. They wanted to write about events closer to home. They thought these events were more important. Historians call this Eastern bias.

Ex-Confederates wrote many books about the war after it ended. The books mainly covered Confederate victories in the East. The authors wanted to draw attention away from Confederate defeats in the West. It made the Confederates look like the victors. It wasn't until the late 1900s that historians began seriously studying the war in the West. They published more complete histories of the war.

THE END OF THE WAR

In the spring of 1865, Confederate general Robert E. Lee's forces were on the run. The Army of Northern Virginia was being chased by US general Ulysses S. Grant's army. The chase followed months

of hard fighting. The
fighting was around the
Confederate capital
of Richmond, Virginia.
Lee had won many
battles during the war.
He was one of the
Confederacy's most
successful generals.
US military leaders
thought they had to
destroy Lee's army to
win the war. On April 9,
Grant defeated Lee's
forces at the Battle
of Appomattox Court
House in Virginia.
Later that day, Lee
surrendered his army
to Grant. Many people

consider that moment the end of the war. However, the war didn't officially end for another year.

Only the Army of Northern Virginia surrendered at Appomattox. It was just one of several Confederate armies. The others continued to fight. In fact, five battles took place after Appomattox. The Battle of Palmito Ranch was the last major clash of the war. It took place in Texas between May 12 and 13, 1865.

Violence continued after the Battle of Palmito Ranch. Bands of guerrilla fighters attacked soldiers and citizens. They also raided towns. These bands were made up of ex-soldiers, army deserters, and civilians. Some bands were loyal to the Confederacy. Some were loyal to the United States. Others were made up of outlaws. Both the North and the South considered guerrilla fighters criminals, not soldiers.

The last Confederate general surrendered on June 23 of that year. Organized fighting ended in 1865. But it wasn't until August 20, 1866, that President Andrew Johnson officially proclaimed an end to the war.

Certain facts about the Civil War have been changed or forgotten. These facts include why the South seceded, why the United States fought the war, who fought for the Confederacy, and where the war took place. Civil War myths can hide truths about slavery and make those who supported it look like heroes. Understanding what really happened in the Civil War can help people to better learn from history.

IMPORTANT DATES

1860

Abraham Lincoln is elected president of the United States in November.

1860

In December, South Carolina becomes the first of eleven states to secede from the United States.

1861

The American Civil War begins.

1863

The Emancipation Proclamation goes into effect on January 1. This legally frees enslaved people in Confederate states. The Confederacy does not recognize the proclamation, but the US military can enforce it.

1864

The Confederate city of Atlanta, Georgia, falls to US forces. This success helps President Lincoln get reelected.

1865

General Robert E. Lee surrenders his army to General Ulysses S. Grant at Appomattox Court House, Virginia, on April 9. But this is not the end of the Civil War.

1866

President Andrew Johnson officially declares an end to the Civil War on August 20.

STOP AND THINK

Tell the Tale

Chapter One of this book explains how several states left the United States in 1860 and 1861. Imagine you are in South Carolina's capital on December 17, 1860. You are there for the discussion about leaving the United States. What is it like being there? What is being said? Write 200 words explaining the experience.

Surprise Me

Chapter Four discusses the Civil War in the Western and Trans-Mississippi Theaters. After reading this book, what two or three facts about the western battles of the Civil War did you find most surprising? Write a few sentences about each fact. Why did you find each fact surprising?

Dig Deeper

After reading this book, what questions do you still have about slavery in the United States? With an adult's help, find a few reliable sources that can help you answer your questions. Write a paragraph about what you learned.

Say What?

Studying the Civil War can mean learning a lot of new vocabulary. Find five words in this book you've never heard before. Use a dictionary to find out what they mean. Then write the meanings in your own words and use each word in a new sentence.

GLOSSARY

bias
being for or against one thing, person, or group compared to another

delegate
a person who represents others in government

emancipation
the act of freeing people from slavery

federal
relating to central rather than state government

guerrilla
describing irregular warfare in which a small group uses surprise attacks and property damage to fight against a larger force

morale
the mental and emotional state of a group of people

pension
a regular payment from the government after performing a service

regiment
a unit of troops in an army

secede
to formally withdraw from an organization

theater
an area of action, especially in a war

ONLINE RESOURCES

To learn more about the facts and fiction of the Civil War, visit our free resource websites below.

Visit **abdocorelibrary.com** or scan this QR code for free Common Core resources for teachers and students, including vetted activities, multimedia, and booklinks, for deeper subject comprehension.

Visit **abdobooklinks.com** or scan this QR code for free additional online weblinks for further learning. These links are routinely monitored and updated to provide the most current information available.

LEARN MORE

Harris, Duchess, and Samantha S. Bell. *The Thirteenth Amendment and Its Legacy*. Abdo Publishing, 2020.

Jarrow, Gail. *Blood and Germs*. Calkins Creek, 2020.

INDEX

About the Author

Ryan Gale is a Minnesota-based artist and writer. He enjoys reading and writing about history.